P9-CBQ-916

A Home for the Winter

By Mr. O'Beirne's 2nd Grade
Stoddert Elementary
Washington, DC

Scholastic Inc. New York Toronto London Auckland Sydney Mexico City New Delhi Hong Kong Buenos Aires

ORIGINAL COVER

MEET THE AUTHORS

Back left to right: Ares Brown, Clara Eriksson Clay, Merritt Claud, Rory Biggs, Emma Ludgin, Riley Tennyson, Daris Lohja, Peter Hayes, Luca Strohl, Eleanor Rosser, Josephine Schneider, Isabelle Boiko
Front left to right: Levi Godzwa, JanChriz Pena, Nano Nikuradze, Olga Cherkashina, Tomas Portilla-Marchiori, John Dausch, William Floman, Jacob Opsitos, Nikita Kuzovenko, Alejandro Gomez, Valeria Drobinina

Eagle was confused. Searching the ground as he flew south over the snowy woods and rocky cliffs along the great Potomac River, he didn't understand why the other animals weren't headed that way, too.

"As the weather gets colder, it's harder for me to find food so I fly to warmer weather. How do the others, like Black Bear and White-Tail Deer, survive the cold winter here? I just wish I could know. If only I could BE a bear so I could find out!"

As Eagle flew, he began to feel a heaviness in his wings and his body began to shake. He felt furry and soft as his white feathers turned to thick black fur and his lightweight bird body turned into a heavy thick body.

Eagle's wings grew shorter and his hind legs grew longer and thicker. He had actually become a black bear! His body felt heavy, yet he floated down like a feather and landed in the soft snow near the frozen water of the Potomac River ... on four paws!

Black Bear sniffed the ground and looked around. He felt a painful hunger in his stomach for fish and berries. So he waddled to the shore of the frozen river to catch a tasty meal. He ate his fishy fill by the river for many days. He began to notice that each day seemed to be shorter than the one before it, and colder, too. And he was growing bigger!

After all that eating, Black Bear began to feel slow and sleepy. He felt a strong urge to curl up in a cozy cave in the cliff by the river and fall into a deep sleep. And so he did.

The sleep seemed to go on and on for many weeks. And as he slept, he dreamed about the other animals in the forest and what they were doing. He worried about White-Tail Deer. How could he survive the cold without finding a cozy cave as he had?

As Black Bear dreamed, his body began to shake. He was shrinking as his color grew lighter. He felt antlers beginning to grow out of his head and he felt his paws turn into hooves and his legs stiffen as he sprung up on all fours.

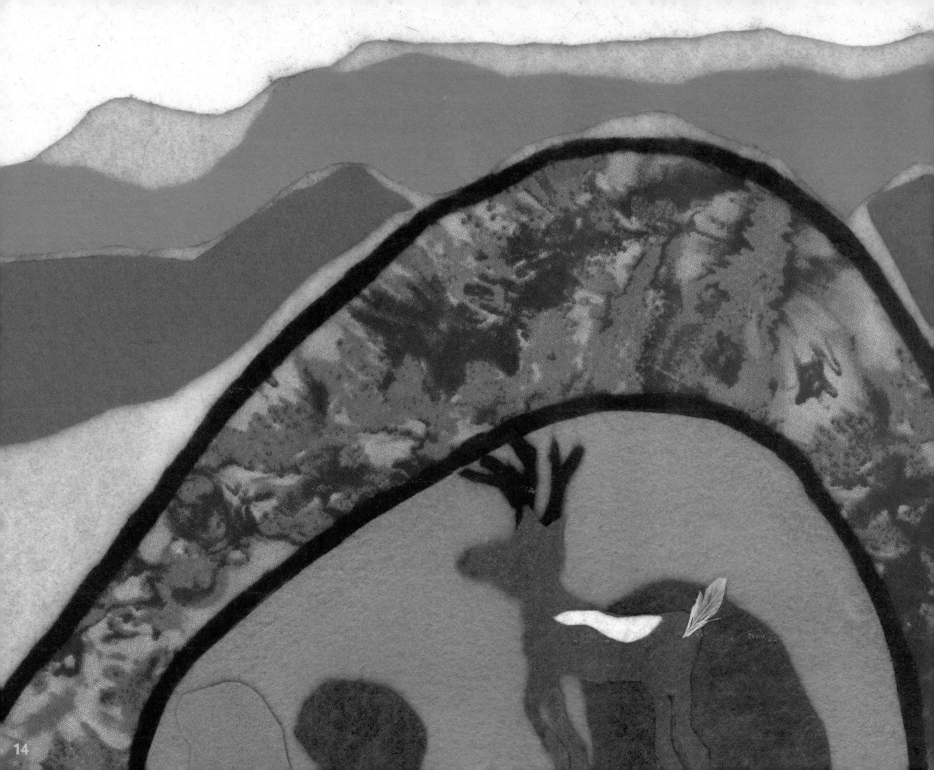

He had become a white-tail deer! At once, White-Tail Deer stepped gracefully out of the cave. He wandered over to snack on sugar maple and dogwood tree buds. As he munched, he noticed a small grove of pine trees. The boughs were covered in snow and sheltered the cozy space beneath them from the winter winds.

"Ah," he said, "that looks like just the kind of comfortable spot to become my home for the winter. I shall leave in the morning to search for food, and come back to my grove to rest."

After falling asleep in his new tree shelter, White-Tail Deer dreamed of flying over open woods and water. He thought, "How I wish I could be like Eagle and fly freely to warmer weather!"

At once, his body began to shake ferociously. It began to feel lighter, as though it might be floating above the ground. He noticed a strong urge to flap what were once his legs and hooves. But no longer. White-Tail Deer suddenly woke to find that he had taken the shape of an eagle!

Eagle tested his wings and found them to be quite satisfactory. He flapped and flapped until he was once again soaring high above the Potomac River.

"It's so GOOD to be free to fly once again!"

When he searched the ground below, he was pleased to spot Black Bear fishing by the river and White-Tail Deer returning to her cozy grove, heavy with a recent meal. But this time, there was no snow on the pine boughs. While Eagle dreamed, the days had become longer and the sun shone directly overhead.

Spring had come! And now Eagle knew that he did not have to worry about the others surviving the winter ever again. They knew how and they had done just fine.

THE END

Kids Are Authors®

Books written by children for children

The Kids Are Authors® Competition was established in 1986 to encourage children to read and to become involved in the creative process of writing.

Since then, thousands of children have written and illustrated books as participants in the Kids Are Authors® Competition.

The winning books in the annual competition are published by Scholastic Inc. and are distributed by Scholastic Book Fairs throughout the United States.

For more information:

Kids Are Authors® 1080 Greenwood Blvd.; Lake Mary, FL 32746 or visit our web site at: www.scholastic.com/kidsareauthors

All rights reserved. No part of this publication may be reproduced, or stored in a retrieval system, or transmitted in any form or by any means, electronic, mechanical, photocopying, recording, or otherwise, without written permission of the publisher.

For information regarding permission, write to Scholastic Inc., Attention: Permission Department, 557 Broadway; New York, NY 10012.

Copyright © 2014 by Scholastic Inc.

Scholastic and associated logos are trademarks and/or registered trademarks of Scholastic Inc.

ISBN 13: 978-0-545-80578-0   12 11 10 9 8 7 6 5 4 3 2 1

Cover design by Bill Henderson

Printed and bound in the U.S.A.   First Printing, June 2014